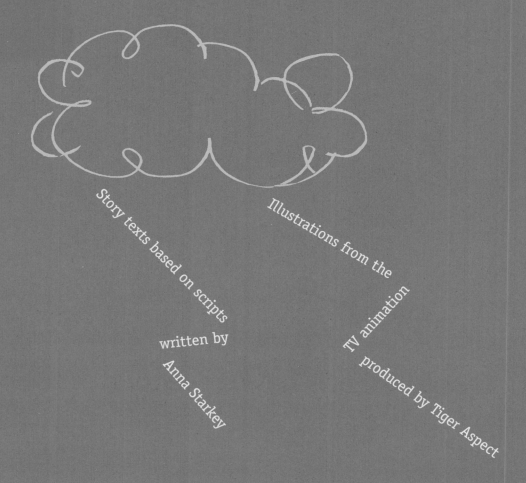

Story texts based on scripts

written by

Anna Starkey

Illustrations from the

TV animation

produced by Tiger Aspect

PUFFIN BOOKS
Published by the Penguin Group: London, New York, Australia, Canada,
India, Ireland, New Zealand and South Africa
Penguin Books Ltd, Registered Offices: 80 Strand, London WC2R 0RL, England

puffinbooks.com

First published 2009
Text and illustrations © Lauren Child/Tiger Aspect Productions Ltd, 2009
The Charlie and Lola logo is a trademark of Lauren Child
All rights reserved
The moral right of the author/illustrator has been asserted
Made and printed in Italy

ISBN: 978-0-141-38473-3

characters created by

lauren child

My really BIG Charlie and Lola ANNUAL 2010

This ANNUAL **belongs** to:

PUFFIN

Contents

I have this little sister Lola.
She is small and very funny.
Lola is always very extremely busy painting,
bouncing, skipping, sticking, playing...

The VERY best people to play with

Lotta is Lola's very **best** friend in the whole wide world and school. Lotta and Lola love to play **pretending** games. Sometimes they are circus people who can do **acrobat-ing** and sometimes they are **doctors** who can make ill people better.

Lotta

Soren Lorensen is Lola's **imaginary** friend. He always wants to play with Lola, which is especially good when everyone else is too busy to do **playing**.

Soren Lorensen

Morten is Marv's brother and he really likes the **round-and-round** game best. Lola secretly thinks that it is a tiny bit boring, but she plays it with Morten anyway because it is his **favourite**.

Morten

Charlie

Marv

Marv is my **best** friend and we really like playing **football** together and going for **bike** rides. Marv and me have some good **pretend** games too, like **Captain Squidbones** and the pirates!

Sizzles

Sizzles is Marv's sausage dog. He likes any kind of game, especially chasing **birds** and running about. He can also do very good **tricks**.

(Draw a picture of yourself HERE!)

This is **me!**

My **favourite** game is:

....

The **people** I like to play with are:

....

....

The **things** we like to play are:

....

....

PLAYTIME is the best!

Lola says,
"Playing indoors is actually my FAVOURITE.

I can play dressing up...

or paint pictures...

or do leaf prints...

and I can even have
a special INDOORY picnic
with you, Marv and Lotta!"

And I say,
   "But there are also good games to play outside too –

like bouncing and boinging...

skipping...

bike rides...

and the
race-around-
the-park game.

And you know, Lola, Sizzles likes being outside better
   than anything in the whole wide WORLD.
   You do like to play with Sizzles, don't you?"

"Yes, yes, YES!
I completely DO, Charlie.
   OK – let's do a little bit
of EACH kind of playing!"

I WENT to the mOOn...

This is one of Lola's ESPECIALLY favourite games.

You have to pretend that you are going on holiday to the moon, and you take it in turns to think of funny things to bring.

Lola might say, "I went to the moon, and I took a big green jelly!"

Then I might say, "I went to the moon, and I took a big green jelly and... a giraffe!"

Then Lola might say, "I went to the moon, and I took a big green jelly and a giraffe, and a football!"

You can play too – you just
need to keep thinking
of **things** to bring, and **remember**
what the other person has said.
You can play it with two
people, or with **lots** of people.

Write a list of things
YOU would like to
take to the **moon**:

9

Thunder COMPLETELY does NOT scare me

I have this little sister Lola.
She is small and very funny.
One thing that Lola is VERY
scared of is storms.

"No, I'm NOT,
Charlie!"

"Then why have
you got cushions on
your ears, Lola?"

"Because I AM NOT scared...
but my ears might be!"

So I say,
"Well, if you're not scared of storms
then why are you hiding
behind the sofa?"

"Because, Charlie,
I'm doing...
behind-the-sofa playing!"

"Lola, why don't we play a game,
    to help you forget the storm?"

"I really ACTUALLY like storms, Charlie,
    but we can play a game if you like."

But when we hear a BIG

r u m b l e

of thunder
Lola says...

14

"AHHH!"

And I say,
"You ARE frightened, Lola."

"No, I'm not, Charlie.
Not even a
TEENY bit!"

At lunchtime we hear another
loud **bang!**

"AHHH!"

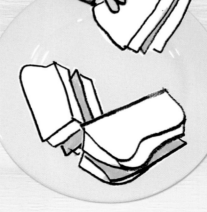

16

"Charlie,
I
really
think
the
sky
is
falling
down.

"There is a big
giant
stamping on it

and he is extremely

CROSS because his tummy is rumbling.

I think he might be hungry...
maybe we should give
him our sandwiches!"

"There isn't a giant, Lola,
it's just **thunder**.
If you watch the storm
then it's not so scary.
Look at the HUGE
raindrops on the window."

Then I say,
"We can have a
raindrop-race."

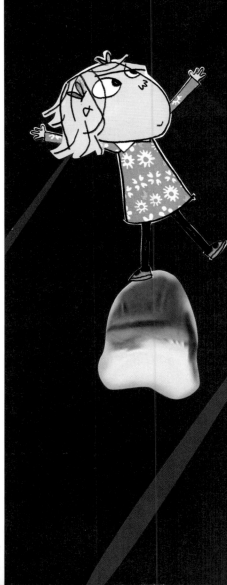

"I'm winning!"
says Lola.

"And when the rain freezes," I say, "it turns into **hail**. Look!"

"Ooh!" says Lola. "It's all **bouncy**."

Then I pretend
to be a weather presenter.

"Welcome to the weather!" I say.

"Here is our street...
and this is
where we live.

Today, we might
have **sun**...

or maybe **rain**...

or **hail**.

We might also
have **lightning**.

And perhaps we might even get

THUNDER!"

23

"I still don't like thunder,"
says Lola.
"It is too LOUD and too SCARY!"

"Don't be scared, Lola.
Have a biscuit – Mum's made
them specially
to cheer you up."

bang!

"AHHH!"

25

"You can stop **banging**, Lola. The storm has stopped.
The **thunder** has gone away."
"Oh, but I LIKE t^hu_nd_{er}, Charlie.
I'm absolutely NOT frightened
of t^hu_nd_{er} now!"

I really absolutely NEED...

Use your ever-so-good **stickers** to help Charlie, Lola, Marv and Lotta prepare for all sorts of EXTREMELY different **weather**! What do you think they **need**?

Charlie and Marv have built a **snowman**.

Lola loves playing on the **beach**.

And Lotta is
splashing in
the puddles!

29

EXTREMELY very interesting
weather FACTS

Did you know that the
Antarctic is the **coldest**
place in the world?
Even colder than
inside our freezer!

"We would be all frozen up,
just like **snowmen**, Charlie!"

Some scientists say
that we can **smell** rain
coming – that the extra
moisture in the air makes
our noses more **sensitive**.

And did you know that a lightning bolt
is a giant spa

Now YOU can
fill in your **own**
FACTS!

"YES, YES, YES...
my **nose** is
as good as Sizzles!"

"I don't want to ever
never be near
one of THOSE
sparklers, Charlie!"

of electricity?!

The **coldest** day this week
was ——————

The **hottest** day this week
was ——————

The most **rainiest** day
was ——————

WEATHERY nOises

Lola can make
a noise just like
thunder using her special tea tray.
But there are other
good weather noises that you
can make!

bang!
crash!

Rattly hailstones

Put some dried peas or lentils in
an empty washing-up liquid bottle.
Make sure it is clean
and dry first! Then shake it
up and down to make
a very loud hail noise.

rattle

rattle

Raindrops

Use a xylophone to
make a **pitter-patter**
noise like **raindrops**.

plink

plink

Whooshy wind

Take a large piece of stiff card
and hold it up in the air.
All you need to do now is **shake** it
up and down to make a **wind** sound.

swishy-swooshy

And to make a really **loud** whistly wind
noise just like in a **storm**,
roll up the cardboard into a big **tube**
and blow through it very hard!

But Marv is ABSOLUTELY Charlie's best friend

I have this little sister Lola.
She is small and very funny.
Lola has made pink milk for Marv and me –
we are busy watching our favourite TV programme,
Captain Squidbones!

"I never want to see your ugly fishface again! Arrrh."

"Oh, the programme's finished," Marv says.
"I wish we could watch Captain Squidbones all day!"

"So do I. I have got to go to the library with Dad now, but maybe we could play Squidbones in the garden later?"

"What happened?"
Lotta says.

"Charlie?"

In the kitchen, Lola says,
"I have ever NEVER heard Charlie
and Marv be cross before EVER."

"Maybe we should get Charlie
        and Marv to do a
    making-up hug, Lola?"

        "I don't think
Charlie and Marv do
    making-up hugs, Lotta."

And then Lola says,
        "I know! Let's make
Marv a making-up card...
        we can make it so
Marv thinks it's
        from Charlie.
And then they'll make up!"
        "Yes, yes, yes!"
    says Lotta.

After posting Marv's card,
    Lola says,
        "Mum says we can
go to the shop for ice cream."

Later at the shop,
Lola whispers,
"**Look!**
It's Marv.
Come on, let's hide!"

Marv says,
"Let's get these biscuits!
I love these."

40

"Who is that boy, Lola?"

"I don't know."

"Well, they're definitely BEST friends because
   they like the same
biscuits," says Lotta.

"OH NO!
Marv has a NEW best friend."

And Jack says,
   "They're my best too.
You like the same
      things I do!"

Back home, Lola says,
"Maybe the card
didn't work,
what else can we do...?"

"Charlie could give him lots of popcorn!" says Lotta.

And Lola says,
"Yes, but I don't really
know where to get EVER so much popcorn."

"What about dogs?" says Lotta.
"We know Marv likes dogs."

"But Marv already
has Sizzles," says Lola.

Finally, Lola says,
"I know! We could make an
actual pirate treasure chest."

"That is a very
good idea, Lola!"

Later, Lotta says, "Oooh, it looks very pretty."

"Yes!" says Lola. "Let's find Charlie,
so he can give the treasure chest to
Marv actually himself."

Then Marv shouts back, "Catch that rotten rascal!"

"Hah-ha, got you, Pirate Charliebones! Now give us the treasure!"

Then we see a treasure chest. And I say, "Did you bring that treasure chest, Marv?"
"No, did you, Jack?"
"No, I didn't."

"Arrrh, then it's mine! Get your hands off MY treasure," says Jack.

And I say, "No, the treasure is mine... ALL mine!"

And Marv says, "You good-for-nothing jellyguts!"

Then Lola and Lotta shout,
"STTTOOOOOPPP!"

"Charlie is not a jellyguts!" says Lotta.
And Lola says,
"He's your actual best friend!"

Then Morten comes along.
"Look, Marv, this card came for you while you were out."

"Dear Marv,
You are my FAVOURITE and my BEST.
Love, Charlie."

"Did you write this, Lola?"

"Yes, it was me pretending
to be Charlie.
And we made the treasure
for you too."

Then Marv says,
"Oh, Lola, did you
think that me and Charlie
were not best friends
any more?"

"Yes," says Lola.

So I say, "But Lola, we are the best friends ever.
We've just been playing Squidbones."

Lola says, "Are you definitely COMPLETELY sure?"

And Marv says, "Definitely, Lola.
Of course Charlie is my best friend.
BESTEST friends."

"Phew!" says Lola.

"Now hand over the treasure!" shouts Marv.
And we all say,
"Arrrh, **never**, you good-for-nothing
jellyguts!"

How to have a **pirate** PARTY

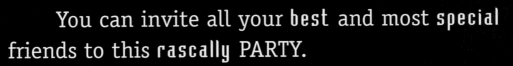

You can invite all your **best** and most **special** friends to this **rascally** PARTY.

Pirate costumes

You could ask your friends to come dressed as **pirates**! Here are some very good ideas for their **costumes**.

If you can find an old-fashioned **hat**, you could stick on some **piratey** gold bits.

Ask a grown-up or biggish person to help you make a **sword** and an **eye patch** out of card.

Tie a roguish coloured **scarf** on your head.

Wear a **stripy** T-shirt, or a waistcoat and an old worn shirt to look extra **raggedy**.

Trace the SKULL and **crossbones** below and use it as a template to
make your very own Jolly Roger. When you've finished, just attach
the flag to a **stick** using sticky tape and you're ready to be a **pirate!**

Wrap this section round your stick or twig

EXTREMELY yummy snacks for your pirate PARTY

Chocolate barnacle BITES

You will need:

50g (1¾oz) dark chocolate

20g (1oz) puffed rice cereal
   or cornflakes

mixing bowl

big spoon

six paper cake cases
(and a grown-up to help!)

1 Ask your grown-up to melt the **chocolate**, then stir in the **cereal** and mix it up!

2 Spoon a little bit of the **mixture** into each of the cake cases and leave them to cool. You can put them in the fridge to set if you are in a hurry!

Smuggler's PUNCH

Mix some of your favourite **fruit** juice with some water. You can add chopped grapes and slices of apple to make it extra fruity!

SCARY vegetable sea monster

You will need:

big plate

vegetables

(including celery sticks,
red peppers,
carrots and apples,
and a grown-up to do the chopping!)

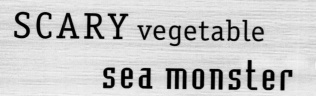

1 Arrange the celery sticks around the top of the plate to make **monster** hair.

2 Use two pieces of cauliflower to make **ears**.

3 Use small pieces of pepper as your monster mouth, and add scary **teeth** with ziggy-zaggy pieces of apple.

4 Make scales from slices of cucumber. Finish off your monster using two peas and slices of carrot to make **eyes** and a slice of carrot for the **nose**.

Charlie's pirate FACTS

Yo, ho, ho! Charlie knows some SUPER scurvy facts about these seafaring scoundrels.

Pirates like Captain Squidbones were often at sea for months and didn't have many **tasty** things to eat. They had to eat just **biscuits** and **eggs** unless they caught some **fish**.

"Didn't they have **pink** milk, Charlie?"

Captain Blackbeard was a **real** pirate and one of the most frightening. He tied burning candle wicks into his long, black **beard** to make himself look even more **scary**.

" I think I would be a much more scarier **pirate!**"

There were around 80 **pirates** on each pirate **ship** and every one got an equal share of any treasure or **booty**.

"Yes, Charlie, sharing is good. You can have the **purple** sweets."

And here are some really very good pirate JOKES:

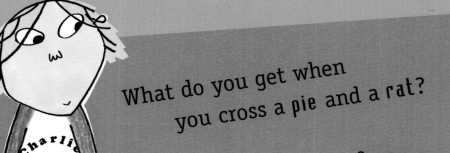

What do you get when you cross a pie and a rat?

Pie Rat!

What's every pirate's favourite dessert?

Jelly Roger!

What's a pirate's favourite food?

Fish and Ships!

Why couldn't the pirate play cards?

Because he was sitting on the deck!

Who's going to ⸺k the plank?

58

Pirate STICKER scene

Charlie, Marv and Jack are playing **Captain Squidbones**!
Give them some **piratey** hats and swords.

Add Lotta and Lola –
they want to be
pirates too!

What lives in the water?

Make your own BEST friends CARD

Cut out one of the **cards** on the next
page to send to your very BEST **friend**.
You can colour it in, and maybe
add some **especially** good
stickers, glitter, pretty paper
or even feathers.

Thanks for
being my
completely
BESTEST
best friend!

For a VERY
special
best friend!

My BEST bestest friend

Draw your BEST friend here!

My BEST friend's name is ....

I met my BEST friend at ....

Some SPECIAL things that we like doing together ....

....

....

"I've been completely EVER so busy, Charlie –
playing with my most favourite toys and sticking
and painting and lots of other extremely good things!"
And I say,
"That's good, Lola, but who's going to clear up all this mess?"
And Lola says,
"It's not messy, Charlie. It's just all spread out!"